SHORT ACCOUNTS OF TRAGIC OCCURRENCES

NICK McARTHUR

SHORT ACCOUNTS OF
TRAGIC OCCURRENCES

LIVRES
DC
BOOKS

Cover illustration by Alain Pilon.
Author photograph by Derek Evans.
Book designed and typeset by Primeau Barey, Montreal.
Edited by David McGimpsey for the Punchy Writers Series.

Copyright © Nick McArthur, 2009.
Legal Deposit, Bibliothèque et Archives nationales du Québec
and the National Library of Canada, 1st trimester, 2009.

Library and Archives Canada Cataloguing in Publication
McArthur, Nicholas, 1984-
Short accounts of tragic occurrences/Nicholas McArthur.
(Punchy prose)
Short stories.
ISBN 978-1-897190-51-7 (bound)
ISBN 978-1-897190-50-0 (pbk.)
I. Title. II. Series: Punchy prose
PS8625.A784S46 2009 C813'.6 C2009-901786-5

For our publishing activities, DC Books gratefully acknowledges the financial
support of the Canada Council for the Arts, of SODEC, and of the Government
of Canada through the Book Publishing Industry Development Program (BPIDP).

Canada Council   Conseil des Arts
for the Arts   du Canada

Société
de développement
des entreprises
culturelles
Québec ✦✦

Printed and bound in Canada by Groupe Transcontinental. Interior pages
printed on 100 per cent recycled and FSC certified Enviro Print white paper.
Distributed by Lit DistCo.

DC Books
PO Box 666, Station Saint-Laurent
Montreal, Quebec H4L 4V9
www.dcbooks.ca

To Stephen Beecroft,
for St. Crispin's Day

CONTENTS

SHORT ACCOUNTS OF
TRAGIC OCCURRENCES

1

Mr. Bloomer boiled the eggs and mashed them in a large bowl. He added mayonnaise and chopped onions, stirred the mix, buttered the bread, and died before lunchtime. The sandwich, uneaten, lay on the table. The mayonnaise was full of regret, and the eggs never said goodbye to their mother. The onions cried.

2

"Darling, I am a flag-ship full of holes without you. My shipmates are all Republicans who tell jokes about their wives. My captain is a chimpanzee. Seriously, just pay me the alimony."

3

Mary-Jane Somerville, drunk, sixteen, and full of Taco-Tent enchiladas from the Sayreville Mall food-court, purchased a new nose-ring and a white vinyl belt, and wore them the entire month of February. Her mother, egregiously, did not see it coming.

COMMENTS HEARD AROUND THE WORLD
IN THE HOURS BEFORE IT ENDED

(OR: HOW I LEARNED TO STOP
WORRYING AND LOVE SCI FI)

Somewhere in the Pacific, off the Coast of China:
"Admiral, you are absolutely positive that you're cool to steer this thing, right? Because we can just call Hollander up from the lower deck, and he can guide this tub in, and no one has to even know about the flaming Sambuca and absinthe shots on what has otherwise been a pretty finely executed covert op. So, yeah–you're cool, right? Just be cool, man. Be cool."

Metropolitan Los Angeles Area:
"Colleen, I think you've been watching too many reports on incompetence in the military. Honestly, a four star admiral so disaffected and lonely and catatonically dead inside that he gets drunk, then renounces his country, and then rams a submarine full of biological weaponry into Shanghai harbor? Where did you come up with this? You know, ever since you stumbled into that top secret radiation booth, it's like you think you're psychic or something.... So what if I was just thinking about your sister? It's her birthday next month."

Sayreville County:
"Aren't you just Mama's special little baby? Aren't you the apple of my eye? No more turning tricks and getting high for Mama! Me and you, we are going to have a happy life together–aren't we pumpy-kins? We are going to have a long, long, long, long, and happy life! Oh yes we are! *Oh yes we are!*"

Meanwhile, Back off the Coast of China:
"Okay now, dude–Admiral–let's just straighten ourselves out, man. Because, we're coming in kind of crooked right now. Maybe if we just went, like, ninety degrees in either direction, you know? As in, left? As in, the opposite of what we're doing right now? Oh, so now we're accelerating. Okay, sure thing, Admiral. You're the boss, man. I feel like I've got to tell you though, Sir, I'm not a hundred percent certain I can get behind you on this. In fact, I feel like this may be the total opposite of what we should be doing right now, safety-wise. But I can see by that glint of madness in your eyes that you don't fully agree with me. I can totally respect that. I can understand where you're coming from on this. But maybe if we could just talk this out and come to some kind of compromise? Like, maybe something everyone could live with? You know what I mean? You know what I'm saying, here, Admiral?"

The Outskirts of Shanghai:
"Fireworks! Fireworks! Fireworks! Fireworks! Fireworks! Fireworks! Yay!"

The White House Master Bedroom:
"Mr. President, I'm sorry to wake you, Sir, but we have some, let's just call them decreasingly anomalous reports of total horror and mass death in Shanghai. Also, it sounds like US Navy may be at least *tangentially* to blame for this whole thing. No Mr. President, I'm not sure where your pants are. The Chinese ambassador is here and he is frankly pretty steamed up. No Sir, I wasn't trying to be funny. Yes, I know how much those people enjoy their steamed rice. Well, I imagine our first move is to find those pants, Sir."

In A Fortified Compound Somewhere in the Nevada Mountains, Fitted with Satellite Dishes and Machine Gun Turrets and a Full Stock of Iodine Pills and a Gas Generator, and About a Century's Worth of Canned Asparagus and Spam and Alphaghetti and Other Such Goods:
"You call that a bowline? That's not a bowline. That's nothing like a bowline! You little bastards wouldn't know how to survive a nuclear holocaust if your father was Daniel Boone and your mother was that juiced-up transvestite from the *Terminator* movies!"

Las Vegas, Nevada:
"I absolutely will marry you. Yes! Your name's Becky, right? Yeah, I thought so. Mine's Stan. Have I told you about my time machine yet, Becky? Because I have a time machine. Typically I only use it for good, but I've got to be honest with you–there's a fair chance I'm going to come back from the future and stop myself from marrying you. Oh–yep–yep–yep–here I come right now. Right over there, storming up here to stop myself. Well, I guess I'll see you later, Becky. I've got to do whatever I tell me to do."

The Surprisingly Homey White House Kitchen:
"Mr. President, I'd like to introduce you to Mr. Wei Ling Chan, the PRC's ambassador to the United States. Now before we start, can I get you gentlemen some drinks? Maybe a light snack or an American cup of coffee? Some Valium, perhaps? Please, Ambassador Chan, there's really no need to cry. Here, have a tissue. Have a handkerchief. Here, have a little Valium. Now, you say you're entire family was in Shanghai at the time of the explosion? Well, maybe they made it out in time. What's that? You've already confirmed reports that they definitely did not make it out in time and that their deaths were especially horrific? Here, have some pretzels. Have some candied nuts. They're butterscotch flavor."

Zhongnanhai (Presidential Residence), Beijing:
"General Tso, what's the death toll in Shanghai? Mmhmm, mmhhmm. Yes, that *is* high. And the toxic fog is still spreading? Mmhmm. And the Americans are responsible? One rogue Admiral acting alone, you say? And his name was Admiral Bludgeldt? Admiral Bludgelt of the US Navy? Yes, I think I saw him on *Makeover Story.* You know, the 'Legends of America' episode, where Dick Cheney starts crying halfway through his pedicure? Yes, it certainly was hilarious, General. What's that? Oh right. Well, let's just bomb them into submission, then."

Meanwhile, Back in the Metropolitan Los Angeles Area:
"Okay, fine. Maybe you *are* psychic, Colleen. Maybe you *can* see the future. Maybe we *are* all going to die in some vast atomic dervish of flames and searing flesh. And sure, Colleen–maybe the few remaining bands of survivors will be made to live like animals, ripping at the iridescent flesh of what used to be their loved ones. But tell me this, Colleen, since you're such a genius–if this is all going to happen so soon, why can't we see any bombs falling yet? Why haven't we heard even a single explosion in the dista–"

Somewhere Just Outside of the Metropolitan Los Angeles Area:
"Fireworks! Fireworks! Fireworks! Fireworks! Fireworks! Fireworks! Yay!"

The St. Louis Channel Four News Station:
"This just in: the entire West Coast, from San Diego to Seattle, has been decimated by atom bombs. The death toll is almost literally mind-boggling. All forms of broadcast communication are down, and will probably never, ever be back up again. Don't hold your breath, people. Don't hold your breath unless in an attempt to

kill yourselves. If you are able to watch this broadcast at all, that probably means you are Jerry, our station manager, or Hector, the Puerto Rican kid who brings me Boston Cream donuts. Also, Jerry–and I only tell you this because the world seems to be ending, and you have always been a good friend to me–Jerry, I slept with your wife at last year's Christmas party and she really seemed to enjoy it. Also, Hector video taped the whole thing and even got to participate a bit. Looking good, Hector!"

The Fortified Compound Somewhere in the Nevada Mountain Range:
"The moment is finally here, folks. Either God or the Devil or some insurgent group of Mid-East bastards has finally come here to put us to the test. Are we frightened? Well, the weakest among us are probably frightened. But will we give in? We wouldn't even dream of giving in if we were vastly outnumbered, totally out-gunned, starved, thirsty, dirty, exhausted, dyspeptic, hungover, and plagued by increasingly volatile bouts of in-fighting. But we all know that that's never going to happen, so let's just go with 'no, we are not going to give in.' Now are there any further questions before I cut into this ham?"

The Not Very Spacious White House Broom Closet:
"Mr. President, I think it may be time we considered actually boarding Air Force One and taking you to a safe location. No, I don't know which location yet, Sir, but your Secretary of Defense has a plan for this event. Sir, I don't think there's much we can do for the Chinese Ambassador at this point. No, no, I never said that I blamed you for his death. Yes, I know that he threw the first punch. I just don't see why you had to discuss his mother in that tone so soon after she'd been nerve-gassed. Sir, of course Buttons can come to the bunker with us, we've already packed his chew toys."

Again, Zhongnanhai (Presidential Residence), Beijing:
"Seattle, check. Portland, check. San Francisco, check. Los Angeles, check. Las Vegas, check. Denver, check. Salt Lake City, check. Poughkeepsie, check...."

Las Vegas—Though Technically Now a Paradimensional Las Vegas Brought About by Multiple Time Paradoxes, and Not at All the Las Vegas We Know and Love, Which Has, By This Point, Been Reduced to a Crater:
"Wait, seriously, where the Hell are we right now? Is this still Las Vegas? Are we in the distant future where the earth is just some dust-swept ball? You know, I was about to get married to the most beautiful call-girl on The Strip, so I think I've got a right to know what's going on here, Future Stan. I mean, what the hell is this place and why does the very fabric of the universe seem to glide on itself like oil on a gentle wave? Are we in Mexico?"

The Soon-To-Be-Evacuated Presidential Residence, (Zhongnanhai) Beijing:
"Boston, check. New York, check. Newark, check. Washington, check. Philadelphia, check. Richmond, check...."

The Thoroughly Defended and Totally Safe, Though Possibly Just a Little Socially Awkward Once You Actually Get Inside of It, Nevada Mountain Compound:
"Listen, no one's going to play Sultan of Sit Downs, or King of the Crapper around here. We should have more than enough toilet paper to last us a few years provided every one conserves and no one goes nuts on arts and crafts night. Let's none of us get too worked up about this, people. There's no need for anyone to start hoarding. Let's just everybody slowly put down our guns and

need your leadership. Oh, and also, the Secretary of Defense is coming and I think he's plotting to kill you. I'm not a hundred percent on this, but just let me just peek-a-boo out the door here and... oh–yep–yep–yep–he is definitely planning on killing you, Mr. President. I mean, he's rubbing two knives together even as we speak. I personally think we need to cut your bath-time short and make good on our escape. Yes, right now. Yes, this very instant. Well, for your own safety, Mr. President. Sir, if Buttons had wanted to escape with us, he wouldn't have played fetch with our enemies."

Once Again, the Miraculously Intact But Dangerously Irradiated St. Louis Channel Four News Station:
"Some shocking developments on the apocalypse front: bombings have ceased, fallout clouds appear to be diminishing, broadcast signals are up, NATO is sending peacekeepers, and I have murdered the entire Channel Four News Team and eaten portions of their kidneys. Now, why don't you guess which one of these five statements is true!"

Paradimensional Las Vegas:
"You're such an asshole."

Inside the Long, Pitch Dark, Ultra Top-Secret Passageway, Ostensibly Leading from the Presidential Bunker to Somewhere in the Outside World:
"No, Mr. President, I can't see anything either. Just a little bit further and we should come to the hatch. Yes Sir, I know that you're frightened. I know you miss Buttons. But I'm right here beside you, Sir. Yes, Mr. President, I do remember how he used to lick between your toes. But we need to keep moving, Sir. It's important

we keep pressing onward or else... or else... or else... or else....
Bingo! I think we've found it, Sir! I mean, I think we're finally at
the hatch! Now all you have to do is walk a few feet forward, and
meet me by the exit, and we can get out of this awful nightmare.
That's right, Sir, just keep walking. Just a little bit further... a little
bit further... further... further.... Don't stop now, Sir... further...
further... further... just a little bit more... a little bit more... further... further... further... further.... Kablamo!

"Oh, what's that, Mr. President? You fell into a chasm, shat-
tering your legs on impact? And you're in unquantifiable pain? And
your mouth is dry? And your muscles are going limp? And you
are rapidly losing both consciousness and blood? Well, how about
that! It's almost like I led you down here, isn't it, Mr. President?
Almost like I led you into a cunning, delicious trap–isn't it, you
hillbilly schmuck? That's right, numb-nuts, *I'm* your Judas! *I'm*
the one who's been plotting your demise! And now the United
States of America is mine and there's nothing you can do about
it! Only it won't be called the United States of America anymore!
From now on, this country will be known as Beatriceland, after
my beloved deaf-mute grandmother. And I will rule it with an iron
fist! No more fetching strawberry shakes for you and Milosovic!
No more cleaning up after Camp David toga parties! From now
on, Goddamn it, *I'm* the top banana! *I'm* the lord and master of
existence! *I'm* the one catching squeeze-jobs from celebrities! All
hail The President, baby! Welcome to Beatriceland, you schmucks!
Break out the caviar! Get some champagne! Ready the guillotines!
I think you're going to like it here!"

SHORT ACCOUNTS OF
TRAGIC OCCURRENCES *(CONT.)*

4

"Yes, I knew Comrade Lieutenant Orlovski; there were few in the camp who didn't. Even when I came to know him–this was years ago now, in Khabarovsk–even then the procedures had begun in earnest. Many of the alterations were admittedly grotesque, though some were charming. It is worth noting Orlovski's absolute willingness in regard the always dangerous and frequently painful procedures. Comrade Lieutenant Orlovski never needed coaxing and was always cheerful. No matter how deformed or monstrously appended he became, Orlovski smiled. It was only years later we discovered the regiment surgeon to be insane."

5

Donald thought the thumbtacks in his shoes must have grown eight or nine inches in the course of the previous week. He meant this metaphorically. "They will shoot up your legs and push out your brains," he thought. "It will probably affect your posture. And also your sex-drive. But, you know, hopefully just the posture."

6

"I am unsure of your flower pattern, Margaret. It strikes me as suspicious and unkind. The lilies are too white. They're like milk spots all over your stomach, and the buttercups, also, make me very uneasy. Once, as a child, I ate a ditch worth of buttercups. I chewed one delicate bell after another until my father came by and said 'Jeremy?' and I vomited. I shall never forget the aroma."

MAKE-A-MONSTER HOME LABORATORY

Sew 'em up, jolt 'em, and watch 'em come alive!
With the Make-a-Monster Home Laboratory,
life is in your hands!
–Excerpted from the now-defunct
Make-a-Monster website, October 2008

CONTENTS
Work Bench
Overhead Lights
100% Organic Animal Parts (assorted)
Hacksaw
Needle and Thread
Tesla Coil Capable of Five Megavolts of Output
INGREDIENT X™ Reanimating Compound (100 oz.)
Safety Goggles
–Excerpted from the back of the Make-a-Monster
Home Laboratory Box Set, December 2008

(What follows is a partial transcript from the proceedings of The
People of Sayreville County vs. The Make-a-Monster Toy
Company, May 2009)

Well... that was some speech, wasn't it ladies and gentlemen?
I mean, that certainly was impressive. I'd like to commend the
prosecution, here, on both their well-wrought vitriol and their over-
active imaginations. But why don't we look at the facts, shall we?
My clients never "claimed for themselves the fearsome powers of
God," and they certainly didn't "cheapen and debase the mysteries

of creation." My clients are *toymakers,* ladies and gentlemen. They produce *playthings* for a living, and they do it extremely well. As a corporate entity, their purpose has been to engage and delight and educate our children, and they've achieved this purpose with distinction and ingenuity. They are *not* "a bunch of Geppettos-turned-Mengeles."

Now, I can understand your concerns. Yes, there have been some incidents. Yes, a number of people have died. Yes, by its very existence the Make-a-Monster Lab seems to rob life of its wonder. I get this, ladies and gentlemen. I'm a Catholic myself. But there is still no reason for anyone here to attack or defame or bankrupt a company whose sole ambition has been the enrichment of our children's lives. Because ultimately—and I cannot emphasize this enough—the Make-a-Monster Toy Company is in no way at fault for the various deaths, maimings, disembowelments, de-facings, de-limbings, defenestrations and so on that have occurred. As I intend to demonstrate, each of these incidents resulted from various customer abuses, and not from any inherent deficiency in the Make-a-Monster product.

Consider:

In the case of the Rodriguez family, young Jorge Rodriguez scoured a local cemetery for additional materials, thereby breaking our terms of use.

In the case of the Dorchester family, twelve-year-old David Dorchester prodded, poked and starved his monsters into vicious displays of gladiatorial combat, also breaking our terms of use.

In the case of the Stinson family, Theodore Stinson tried to fit his head into his monster's jaw, breaking at once our terms of use and the left-most portion of his skull.

In the case of the Lewis family, Davis attempted to breed his monsters using sildenafil citrate and clips from *Animal Planet,* yet again breaking our terms of use.

In the case of the Grabowski family, John stitched his monster to his own left side, making for himself a vile and unholy spectacle of a conjoined twin—which also violated section 2.3b of our terms of use, which clearly states, "the user is not to sew, graft or otherwise bind any monster to any part of his or her person."

And in all of these cases, a parent, grandparent, or other responsible adult was nowhere to be found.

Are you beginning to see my point, ladies and gentlemen? In every single instance, fatalities resulted from negligent parenting, radically unsafe behavior, or some regrettable combination of both. As such, my clients are neither morally at fault nor legally indictable for any of the bizarre tragedies that have occurred. I will say this again: my clients are neither morally at fault nor legally indictable for any of the bizarre tragedies that have occurred.

And when the pivotal moment finally does come, I trust each and every one of you to arrive at a just decision. I trust you all to complete your deliberations, to march straight into this courtroom and say, "We find the defendants not guilty on all one thousand two hundred and ninety three counts of manslaughter."

Thank you.

SHORT ACCOUNTS OF TRAGIC OCCURRENCES *(CONT.)*

7

Jasper was ordinarily kind to the handicapped and did not believe in pushing them in baby carriages, or in sticking them behind bushes. He thought they should be made to feel as normal as possible, though he did not like them doing his laundry. He also disapproved of their crutches and wheelchairs, though he knew well enough that their wheelchairs were not their fault but somebody else's, and that their singing on charity Christmas specials was the best that they were capable of. They practiced for long hours for those charity specials. They worked hard laundering his socks and folding his dress-shirts. They were born disadvantaged with crutches and wheelchairs, and they did not like to be stuck behind bushes. Jasper was ordinarily unkind to the handicapped.

8

"Sesame seeds, cranberry dressing, people falling off of roofs; candied yams and the joys of family, and children get mauled by pets; ham, turkey, squash, bacon, colorectal cancer. Oh, and pumpkins. Let's nobody forget about the pumpkins."

9

On his second last day of stopping for pedestrians, Joseph, the Sayreville County bus driver, happened upon a bird pecking at another bird's eyes–the sight of which was still considerably less unpleasant than the constant and exhausting grinding to a halt for pedestrians.

BUTTERMILK

There were three young men living in the upstairs apartment and all of them belonged in hell. There was an invitation that Mr. Bloomer wasn't sure of. There was a promise of gin. There was a promise of music. There was a promise of something grand you couldn't even think of if you held your breath. It had come to that. Invitations were getting thin.

Mr. Bloomer was old and not above dying. He could die this evening or he might die tomorrow evening. He might die later on next week or not at all. He felt old enough not to die at all, but actually he wasn't. If he wasn't going to pass-on this evening, he thought he might attend the party with the three young men upstairs who belonged somewhere in hell. He dressed in mauve and said, "mauve," into the mirror. He left his apartment and climbed the stairs; knocked on the door and waited.

A man in a blue tie opened it, said, "welcome, welcome, welcome," and patted Mr. Bloomer on the back. The apartment was immense. It spanned into a long, twilit horizon, where sea crabs and sea light danced on the green rocks. In the foyer there was yellow, there was green, there were wretched faces. A fellow with a pink tie and a chin shaped like a shoe box was pulling dollar bills from the top of an open piano. He bundled them in nines and wrapped them in Saran Wrap. Then he threw them at a fan. The money exploded and the man in the pink tie cheered. He glanced over at Mr. Bloomer, who stood dumbly looking on. The man said, "You're never gonna get rich just standing there, asshole."

The third man, who had a green tie and no chin at all, drew pictures of his children on the floor. He labored on his hands and knees with colored chalk and a smudged face. He hadn't seen his children in twelve years, had received no letters, had seen no photos, and when he saw Mr. Bloomer he pointed at one of the chalk drawings and said, "Just look how big he's getting! Bigger than his old man soon!"

Mr. Bloomer sat on the chesterfield and waited very selflessly for a drink. He was a little frightened and was thinking how it might be nice to die soon. He waited for something grand to happen that he couldn't even think of if he held his breath. There were no other guests. There was no music. There were no pink lights, dancing animals, or evidences of God Almighty the progenitor of goodness. The first man, with the blue tie, sat on the couch beside him and sighed. He said: "I've been very lonely. I don't think my wife is ever coming back."

"I'm sorry," Mr. Bloomer said.

The man sighed again. "I killed her," he said, "I drowned her in a bath full of buttermilk." He looked very sad for a moment, but did not cry. He looked down at the ground and shuffled his feet together. Then he perked up, drove a finger into the air and said, "Drinks! Now who would like some gin?" and ran out of the room.

Mr. Bloomer lay down on the chesterfield and tucked his head under a pillow. He decided to dream. Mr. Bloomer considered what to dream about and decided on something from another universe, from another realm, from another sphere of being altogether. He decided to dream about something he could not even think of if he held his breath, and set to work on conjuring his cat Dixie drinking milk from a bathtub where the man with the blue tie's wife lay drowned.

The wife was beautiful and blue as ice. Mr. Bloomer began to weep.

Dixie, the old tiger-striped cat with large paws, a large head, and bad hind legs, was clearly disgusted by the weeping. She stopped lapping at the milk and turned to Mr. Bloomer. Still perched on the tub ledge, she said, "Now what in the hell is this about?"

"Oh, never mind him," the dead woman said. "Just, please, darling, don't stop."

SHORT ACCOUNTS OF TRAGIC OCCURRENCES (CONT.)

10

"You mean Comrade Lieutenant *Andreas* Orlovski–*The Monster of Central Television*? Yes, I remember him well. Who in Leningrad did not love this imbecile? I remember how–and this, when I was still only a child–I remember how it felt both cruel and fitting that the one most hideous man in Russia should host our only game-show. This, to me, was the essence of our Party–equality regard-less; equality through compensation; equality, even in adversity. What did it matter that his neck was limp, or his feet were both inverted, or his fingers were technically salmon rolls? What did it matter, when the weight of his words kept our own heads high, and the grace of his hobbling set our very hearts ablaze? I ask you, my friend, though I do not know your name. I ask you: who ever said that greatness required bladder-control?

"That is fascism, Comrade. *Fascism!*"

11

"These toddlers of Hell are set upon me still. I like them, but will never be a part of them. Mother, I beg you: don't leave me in this daycare. Father, I implore you: change me."

12

Though it was generally agreed that stealing and extortion were not, in themselves, depraved or unforgivable–still many of the townsfolk tended to avoid these things, even amid the stresses of tax season.

THE FOODMART LETTERS

Dear Ms. Anonymous,
When I saw you in the produce aisle, squeezing the plums and caressing the bananas, I was overcome with wonder. You are the most beautiful woman I have ever seen.

Do you mind that I call you beautiful? You don't even know me and may very well be frightened of me. I can accept that. I accept it as a product of your beauty, and I accept it as a product of my ugliness. Often, I too become terrified of ugliness. And always, Ms. Anonymous, I'm most frightened of my own.

Yours in Anticipation,
Mr. Anonymous

●

Dear Mr. Anonymous,
I totally hear what you're saying, Mr. Anonymous. And let me just assure you that I have not always been so beautiful, myself. As a teenager, I was often described as "fat," or "hideous," or "chubby," or "porcine," or sometimes even as "the ugliest girl on campus." Modeling school was a difficult time for me.

Once, in the cafeteria, I was pelted repeatedly in the face with donuts while the other children laughed. On another occasion, I was coaxed into making animal noises for ninety seven and one half minutes–the entire duration of *Babe 2: Pig in the City.* On another occasion, I was forced at gun point to eat plate after plate of spaghetti–also in reference to *Babe 2: Pig in the City.* On another occasion, I was jokingly "beaten with an ugly stick," which turned out to be a crow bar. I was really starting to get down on myself.

What I'm trying to say, here, is that you and I are more alike than we appear to be. Though on the outside I may have silken skin, and perky breasts, and an enviable bone structure, on the inside, I too have a varicose nose, and dramatically crossed eyes, and a slack, drooling, unclosable maw, and... whatever that thing is protruding from your forehead. You needn't be so morose, Mr. Anonymous. You are not alone. One day this cruel, cruel world will appreciate your beauty.

Yours Sympathetically,

Ms. Anonymous

●

Dearest Ms. Anonymous,

Varicose nose? Dramatically crossed eyes? I'm so delighted that you remember me!

Do you recall when we first saw each other? I came limping around the corner and out of the canned foods aisle, and there you were–shimmering like foil in the neon lights. You turned your pretty head and looked at me and–as I remember–barely managed to stifle a scream of horror. But you did stifle it, Ms. Anonymous. You did.

Incidentally, the jury is still out on the protrusion you referred to. It is either some kind growth, or a benign cyst, or I am not, biologically speaking, a human being. In any event, hats have always been a struggle for me, and I'd be very much indebted if you could point me in the direction of an accommodating chapeau. Baseball caps are generally too tight, and anything more florid calls attention to my ears. Can you help me, Ms. Anonymous? I'm embarrassed to ask, but you may be my only hope.

Yours Indebtedly,

Mr. Anonymous

●

Dear Mr. Anonymous,
I know how tricky headgear can be, and I've even suffered a little "hat-ache" myself! Like this one time, in modeling school, I wore a bonnet so tight I had migraines for a week. Another time, I went completely bald after trying to model a bear-trap. Another time, I shaved two centimeters from my cranium using a power sander and tweezers. In hindsight, it may not have been worth it.

But to answer your question: of course I will help you! I'm always happy to help! Personally, I would recommend a wide brimmed cowboy hat with tassels and a chin strap. Black is likely best, and you may need to have it custom fitted. I could do a little seam-stressing myself, if you thought you needed a hand. Let me know what you think, Mr. A. I'll be waiting on your reply.

Your Friend,
Ms. Anonymous

●

My Dear, Dear, Dear Ms. Anonymous,
I am overwhelmed. It seems almost impossible that you, a beautiful woman, would help me, a hideous man, to pick out a hat. You're a kind soul.

So when can we put this together? Tonight perhaps? Say, 7:30 at your place? Also, do you think you could perform the necessary tailoring over a candle-lit dinner, with some low romantic music and just enough wine to suspend your better judgment? I make a famous veal cutlet.

Sincerely,
Mr. Anonymous

●

Dear Mr. Anonymous,
Well, veal cutlets certainly are delicious. But on one occasion, in modeling school, I wore a dress made from cutlets for eight straight days during a record-breaking heat wave. On another occasion, I received third degree burns while trying to model a deep fryer. On another occasion, I suffered a stroke.

   Fashion sure has changed!
   Sincerely,
   Ms. Anonymous

●

Dear Ms. Anonymous,
Right.

   So was that a "yes" or a "no" to dinner?
   Sincerely,
   Mr. A

●

Dear Mr. A,
I'm sorry, but I need to be honest with you: I never even went to modeling school. I mean, I'm not a real model. I work as a shop girl at the Sayreville Foodmart, and every time I hear you limping in, I rip off my smock and grope wildly at the produce. I am a liar, Mr. Anonymous. I'm a liar and a deceiver, and I am also in love with you.

   I think of you often—your oblong forehead and compact arms, and your tiny, disproportionate legs. I think of your incredible forthrightness—how you wear your imperfections on your sleeve.

How you never hide your flaws or pretend you're someone you're not. The way I do.

Mr. Anonymous, I am not a model, and–what with your eyes being permanently crossed–I'm probably not as beautiful as you imagine me to be. But if you could find it in your heart to forgive me, I would still love to have dinner with you.

Yours Affectionately,

Ms. Anonymous

•

Dear Ms. Anonymous,

So–just for the sake of clarity–what you're saying, here, is that you are not a model, and you don't have perfect breasts, and this whole encounter does not generally have the air of a certain classic French fairytale, charmingly retold. Is this more or less what you're saying? That you're not entirely perfect? That you have flaws like everyone else? That all things considered, you're kind of plain and unspectacular, and not at all the resplendent vision I'd imagined you to be? And again, Ms. Anonymous, this is just for the sake of clarity.

Your Pal,

Mr. Anonymous

•

Dear Mr. Anonymous,

Yes, that is more or less what I'm saying–I am not a model, and I've never been to Milan, and I occasionally get rashes along the contour of my jaw. I'm sorry I lied to you. Can you forgive me?

Anxiously,

Ms. Anonymous

●

Mr. Anonymous,
It's been weeks and still no word from you. No notes, no letters, no run-ins at the Foodmart. Where are you, Mr. Anonymous? I miss you. Each time I hear the hiss of sliding doors, I rip off my nametag and start teasing my hair seductively, hoping it might be you. But it never is.

Your hat is coming along well. Last Friday evening I bought felt and some tassels and a two foot stretch of twine. I sewed tiny white bells along the contour of the brim–so I'll always hear you coming.

Can we still have dinner? With veal and red wine and music and candlelight? I'll do the cooking, even. I'll do the cooking and then I'll clean up afterward. And we can have cake.

Your Friend,
Vanessa

SHORT ACCOUNTS OF TRAGIC OCCURRENCES (CONT.)

13

Everyone was charged with their own defense, which could mean anything from cutting switches from your belt with which to beat your children, to operating a brothel on the holiest of high holy days. Nevertheless, operating a brothel in order to shame your children, or cutting a belt in defiance of your faith tended to be looked down on–this because, as with most things, someone's motivations would have to be accounted for.

14

In his quieter moments The Eulogist knew for sure: the Applause-O-Meter is the truest form of criticism.

15

"I am the monster, you are the doe. This is what happens: I eat the fawns, you scream a little, I look into your eyes and feel deeply ashamed, then we get into a long, uneventful romance, then we move in together, into my dark lair, then we get married, then we have a few little rug fawns of our own, then some time passes and you start an affair with the ogre next door, who is both taller and better endowed than me, and then, one day, returning from eating villagers, I come into the bedroom and see you on the bed, you and this ogre, twisted together like a single apple cruller, and (I can only assume, here) you, my wife, have *let* yourself get caught like this, have *let* yourself be discovered in some cheap vainglorious try at debasing me, at making me feel less like the monster, out of spite.

And so, then, what do I do? What do I do now upon finding you in bed? I eat our little fawns, is what I do. Because I'm still the monster and you're still the doe. Remember that, Shnookums."

"EFFECTIVE IN FIVE MINUTES"

So I took these extra fast-acting suicide pills, and–this would be a few minutes ago, during the last commercial break–and so far for whatever reason no serious pains, or total loss of muscle function, or blurring of vision, or outright blindness, or paralyzing facial tics, or manic finger-biting, or involuntary couch-humping, or eye-ball-slash-scrotal-slash-rectal numbness or itching or bleeding or anything like that. Also, no involuntary screaming, punching, kicking, biting, or crying. Also, no hair-, limb-, nose-, or testicle-loss. Also, no indigestion. My cock is pretty hard, but that's not necessarily a side-effect. That's probably the chick who plays April O'Neil on the Friday night TV airing of *Teenage Mutant Ninja Turtles: The Movie,* which I am scheduled to die watching in exactly two minutes and twelve seconds… two minutes and eleven seconds… two minutes and ten seconds….

Come to think of it, my left foot and ankle and lower calf are getting pretty tingly, but my guess?–that's from this morning's Jazz Aerobics and Salsa Slam classes, which can strain my glutes pretty good, but which also give me an ass like two crystal balls in a sausage casing. That might've sounded kind of gay, but actually it wasn't.

One minute and forty three seconds… one minute and forty two seconds… one minute and forty one seconds….

And now the left arm, for whatever reason, is twitching upward at two second intervals. There's a very minimal welling of tears along the basin of my left eye. I also have some minor-league heartburn, and a tightening sensation in the throat. At this point, Raphael has been ambushed by the Foot Clan, and has basically just had his whole ass and half-shell handed to him by Shredder.

Raph was, and remains, the moodiest in the group. Leo's the leader. Don is the nerd. Mike is the kindly but mischievous party animal. Splinter is their Sensei rat. Casey Jones is their chronically angry, sports-themed vigilante friend. Who apparently favors a cricket bat. I mean, you've got to feel bad for an American who favors a cricket bat.

Also, now, as in just this very moment, I get a total deflation of last minute's erection—again, probably because of April's marked absence at this particular juncture in the film. Though to be totally honest, it may also be the sudden onset of blindness, or the numbness in my legs, or the fact that I just wet myself. Also, I seem to be paralyzed. And I can't really breathe. And I'm spasming. Luckily, my sense of hearing is still intact, and I take a great deal of comfort in listening to The Turtles as they struggle and battle and overcome and... and... and... well, now I actually am deaf.

Now I actually am deaf and blind and twitching and limp and paralyzed and

SHORT ACCOUNTS OF TRAGIC OCCURRENCES (CONT.)

16

"I only fell in love with the left half of Colleen. It is difficult to explain how this happened. It becomes even more difficult when I consider that it was her right half, and always her right half, that treated me with respect. Why do we do this to ourselves? Why fall in love with the half that spurns us?"

17

"If I were to purchase your land, and then you were to sell that land undermining my official bid, I would hit you. I would hit you in the face so, so hard. And then you would probably cry while I ate peanuts in the sand and sang songs about inflation. Then we'd have ice cream. I would convince you that this world was not in fact a desolate wasteland. I would say, we're okay, baby. Look at that sunrise. Does that look like a sun rising over a desolate wasteland? No way, baby. No way. You and me, we're going to be alright. You and me–we're going to be alright."

18

"I've come here to be told my failings, which are numerous and horrible. I have come to have this done while partaking of my juice. Will you help me, please? Will you enumerate my failings while I sit in rapt attention? I hope that you will. I hope to be understood, intimately, by each of you. I have come here to be hated, and that's what I intend to do. I have come here to be despised, and I certainly... damn it, Billy, stay out of my sand box!"

SAYREVILLE

When I met Dizzy there must have been five, six pancakes stuffed into his mouth. He could barely keep them in. His hands sliced up another one and in went a mouthful. Chew chew chew. A waitress came by and filled his cup with coffee.

"It's simple," he said. "The temple needs someone to round up parishioners. Wear a tie. Sweet talk some losers. I'd do it myself, but people don't trust this mug. Go figure."

I blinked and Dizzy sucked up another pancake. He bent to lick some syrup from the front of his necktie, and a tiny piece of fluff dropped out of his mouth. Outside the diner it was a beautiful morning. I was hungover. The birds were singing and I felt like saying: "Is that the sweet song of the lark I hear? Yeah, well it's ugly and I wish it would shut up." I sipped my water. I have no idea what a lark sounds like.

"It's a cult?" I asked him.

"More like a church," he said.

"What's our theology?"

"Suicide," he said.

"I'm not really into that, Mr. Desmond."

"Call me Dizzy."

"I don't want to die, Mr. Dizzy, Sir."

Dizzy laughed and shook his head. "You idiot," he smiled. "Of course you want to die. Everyone wants to die. Don't you read Freud? Kafka? Danielle Steele? We're all just *aching* to get killed, which is why we've got to move, move, move. There's money to be made on this."

Dizzy scratched his beard and took a long sip of coffee.

"Do I get to wear a robe?" I said.

"Wear whatever you want, pal."

"Call me Hidey," I said.

"Wear whatever you want, Hidey."

●

Dizzy and his organization set me up on a nighttime beat. His organization was his mother. Her name was Mrs. Desmond, and she was an ambitious, ruby-knuckled old Pole, only slightly less hairy than her son, and taller, who dreamt up a mass-suicide goldmine in the middle of a pedicure. That's what she told me. She and Dizzy drove me in their station wagon to Pescado Nuevo Lounge and she said, "Never you mind with the Italians, Hidey. And Poles like us we don't need. Greeks neither. Find the big money. Jews are good 'cause they get bored easy. WASPs too. The drunker the better, okay?"

Dizzy said the robe would have to wait until after we built the parish, and he gave me a suit that was big in the stomach and short in the legs, and that generally made me look like a toddler on Halloween.

Parked outside the lounge he said, "Be suave, Hidey. Be charming."

"Suave. Charming. Right. But aren't you coming in, Mr. Dizzy?"

He looked through the window at the neon sign. "Can't," he said, "they know me here. We'll pick you up at midnight. Bring friends." I got out of the car and was about to go inside when Dizzy rolled down the window and called me back.

"One more thing, Hidey. The Filchers come to this bar sometimes. Ronnie and Daisy Filcher. But you stay away from them, understand?"

"Why's that, Mr. Dizzy?"

"Money. Ideology. What do you care? If I saw Ronnie Filcher I swear I'd throttle him dead, but you–you just stay away, Hide."

He rolled up his window, and away drove the Desmond organization.

●

Pescado Nuevo Lounge was high-ceilinged, mirrored, and gold. Men with gray hair and twitching chins drank cognac at the bar. Women sat at tables drinking flamingo-pink cocktails. I walked in smiling with my hands in my pockets. Suave and charming. I was standing in the middle of the room, wondering where to begin, when a tall woman in a chiffon dress said, "God I *love* that suit! Are you the painter?"

"No," I said, "I'm a disciple of Pastor Dizzy's Transcendentalism. We're trying to build a parish. Want to join?"

She didn't want to join. Robes didn't interest her. Neither did Kafka. Neither did death.

I saw a melancholy fellow at the bar. He was well-dressed, ill-shaven, and alone, so I decided to give him a try.

"Hi there! Want to join my church?"

He took a sip from his drink but didn't look at me. "I'm Buddhist," he said.

"Well, it's actually a temple."

"Oh."

"More like a cult."

"I see."

"So, are you rich? Bored?"

He turned to me and grinned. "I'm both," he said. "But I'm good. Thanks."

I had no money but ordered a drink anyway. This could have turned out badly if a kind, plump debutante hadn't showed up in time to pay for my scotch. She said her name was Thea. She was twenty one and still had braces. Her hair was gigantic and elaborately piled, and her lips were painted a spaghetti sauce orange. She had horrible make-up.

"Jeez," she said, "don't you have any money? What are you doing in a place like *this* if you haven't got cash?"

"I'm looking for parishioners," I said. "I'm sort of like an instrument of God's divine will. Hey, can you buy me another drink?"

"Well, *I'm* looking for suitors," Thea said, flagging the bartender, "Daddy wants me to get married. He doesn't really care to who, as long as they're not too stupid and can keep me out of the house. I told him 'I'm waiting for my one true love,' but he said, 'with hips like that who are you kidding, Thea?' which was an intelligent thing to say. He's a very intelligent man. Cheers."

"Cheers."

"So are you a suitor?"

I thought about it for a moment. She was fat and bubbly and very pleasant to talk to. "I could be," I said. "Would you join my religion?"

"Why not? Another drink?"

"Please."

"Cheers."

"Cheers."

"So, what's it all about," she asked, "our religion?"

I needed to think this over. I rubbed my forehead and thumbed the length of my eyebrows. "Well, it's sort of about God and investing a lot of money," I said. "We get to move in with the Desmonds and eat a lot of pancakes. I'm not too sure, though—it's a pretty new religion. Eventually we die, I think, but not for a little while. Does that bug you?"

"Not really. Cheers."

"Yeah, sure, Cheers. We also get to wear robes."

There was a stage there, and a Mariachi band got up and sang some songs in Spanish. There were three guitar players, a trumpet player, and a gangly-looking blonde guy playing the castanets. They finished a song and then started on another one–this time a love ballad called "Oh Niña Mia!"

"Daddy will be so happy," Thea said. "He's pretty big on religion himself. Hey, can we get married?"

I didn't see why not.

"Children?"

"If there's time," I said, "but they'll die too, probably."

We agreed having children was a bad idea.

By then it was almost midnight and time to go. I asked Thea if she had any friends there she needed to say bye to, and she said she didn't. We sat on the curb outside Pescado Nuevo and waited quietly for the Desmonds. It was a calm, sweet, aromatic night. Birds were singing and I felt like saying, "Is that the sweet song of the nightingale I hear? Yeah, well it's even uglier and I want it to die." I took a deep breath. I have no idea what a nightingale sounds like, either.

Then they came; Dizzy driving and his mother in the passenger seat, wrapped in a beaded black shawl. We climbed in the back and the car sped off. Lights flipped by. The car was starry on the inside, and I could feel Thea's hand on top of mine. She lay down her head and set it in my lap. She was drunk, apparently.

Dizzy smiled at us in the rearview mirror. He said, "So! What is this, our lovely new parishioner's name? What's your name, sweetheart?"

She said, "Thea," and I said,

"We're getting married, Mr. Dizzy? Will you marry us?"

"Honored," he said, and smiled again.

Mrs. Desmond turned her head and started squinting at Thea. She rubbed her forehead. She bit her bottom lip.

"Thea," she said. "Thea, Thea, Thea. What's your last name, Thea?"

Thea said, "Filcher."

The car took a turn, and Dizzy started muttering. We sped up.

Thea turned her head and asked, "When can we get married?"

I said, "Anytime, Sugarplum. Whenever you want. Mr. Dizzy, where are we going exactly?"

"I said no Filchers, Hidey."

Thea giggled and said, "hey can we get a dog? I know we can't have children, but a dog would be nice. We wouldn't have to kill *him*."

"Dizzy, where are we going?"

"A golden retriever," she said. "Or a Newfoundland. I like *big* dogs."

"Where are we going, Dizzy?"

"Maybe a cat too!" she said. "Hey, do we *have* to live in the Desmonds' house? I know you said we had to, but maybe we could live nearby or something. We have money. We could get an apartment."

I looked at Thea and then back to Dizzy. I asked him again where we were going and he still didn't answer me. Mrs. Desmond leaned over and switched on the radio: "Oh Niña Mia!"

I glanced out the window and saw we were leaving town. We were somewhere in the suburbs and there were rows of white houses and wooden lamp-posts and green and black cars tucked neatly in their driveways.

Then the white houses and wooden lamp-posts went away and we were driving through farm country. There were barns, and chicken coops, cornfields and silos.

I decided to sing along with the radio, only I didn't know any Spanish. So I made up some words to go with the tune: "This debutante I know/would fly to Mexico/to play the castanets/and string up marionettes/but she would never go/because I love her so."

Thea laughed and tickled me. "Great song," she giggled. "What a lyricist! What talent! What a warbley voice!" I bent down and kissed her on the cheek. She smiled, and the car stopped. Dizzy cut the radio, and off went "Niña Mia!" I kissed her again. I kissed her again. I kissed her again.

I looked out the window and saw grass and some trees. A little way down there was a wide blue creek with a birch tree toppled over it. Then the lark, the nightingale, the owl, the sparrow. Whatever it was. It sang.

SHORT ACCOUNTS OF TRAGIC OCCURRENCES *(CONT.)*

19

"Orlovski, Orlovski, Orlovski–you mean that literally bent and faceless Russian dude from up in 14b? Like, the guy who listened to *The Price Is Right* at Voice-of-Almighty-God-type decibels? That's him? That's the guy we're talking about here? The guy so twisted and low and horizontally oriented he had to buy, like, a third shoe, and fit it onto his hand with duct tape, hobbling along like a three-legged shiatsu? Is this who we're talking about? The same guy who–I shudder to even mention it–who used to bleed and shed and leak all over the floor, necessitating therefore that I replace the fucking carpets and therefore passed that cost along to my other tenants, who have therefore not stopped bitching to me ever since? Because if this is the Orlovski you're talking about, you tell him Sammy says hello."

20

"I said that brevity was the soul of my penis and no one laughed. Maybe it was too long to work as a punch-line."

GETTING DEPRESSED IN THREE EASY STEPS!

THINGS YOU ARE GOING TO NEED

With a little effort, some depressing music, equally depressing books, tattered clothes, facial hair, stern looks, marijuana, eighty proof alcohol (or in a pinch, the house red), tattoos (optional), piercings (recommended), and greasy hair (imperative, absolutely imperative) you too can overcome banality! These are all simple tricks, of course, but they are the necessary externalities that will, in time, help to guide your *in*ternal transition from pathetically happy dud, to haunted, uneasy dynamo!

Good luck at the tattoo parlor, loser!

STEP 1–CULTIVATING A WORLDVIEW

Now that you have the essential paraphernalia, it is time to establish an outlook of paranoia, contempt, and confidence in life's futility. Now, I know what you're thinking, but don't worry–this is much easier than it sounds! To begin, get a library card. There may be a fee involved, ranging anywhere from two to ten dollars. Pay it, but look angry. And never be afraid to sulk. You may want to yell, "my tax dollars paid for this shit-hole," before storming your way past a circle of wide-eyed third graders.

Once you have your card, head straight to the philosophy section. You are looking for writers who regard mere wakefulness as unbearable agony. Don't know where to start? Try Nietzsche. Find Nietzsche boring? Well, in that case, fuck philosophy! We're way past philosophy here, anyway! After all, who's the aspiring depressive–you, or Nietzsche? Instead of reading, lock yourself in your bedroom and listen to Nine Inch Nails. Oh, and don't forget to burn incense!

STEP 2–HATING YOURSELF AND OTHERS

The key to an attractive character is crushing, crushing remorse. The best way to achieve this is to behave in a selfish, hurtful and irrational manner. Insult everyone. Betray your dearest friends. Do you love your parents? Well never, ever tell them so! Instead, question their validity as guardians *and* human beings. How about a significant other–do you have one? If so, abuse this person emotionally. Undermine his or her accomplishments right in front of his or her family. Dwell on his or her failures. Comment on the vastly superior hotness of his or her best friend. Oh, and if he or she gets upset, be sure to laugh and spit on the floor. Then bring home a prostitute.

Here's a rule of thumb: if an idea seems unthinkably cruel or morally repugnant, DO IT! In no time you will have, 1) alienated everyone in your life, and 2) developed a perfectly healthy hatred of yourself. Both of these things will be absolutely necessary for the next and final stage of your de-escalation.

Now get on out there and victimize, you unconscionable son of a bitch! And remember: cruelty, cruelty, cruelty.

STEP 3–SECLUSION, MASTURBATION, AND CORN FLAKES

By now your family hates you and you wish you were dead: Excellent work! It is now time to distance yourself. In your home city, inquire after the most roach-infested and crack-addicted area. Find a squalid apartment there in a building that–if at all possible–is the seat of an international cartel for the importation of sex-workers. This will serve as an unyielding "shout out" to the virulence of human kind.

In the midst of your squalor, you are going to need:

1) A television and DVD player;

2) Pornographic DVDs (we suggest *The Greatest Whorey Ever Poled*, or *The Greatest Whorey Ever Poled 2: The Second Cumming*);

3) Photographs and Other Memorabilia of the Life You Might Have Had (the happier the memories, the more soul-crushing);

4) Alcohol and Other Intoxicants (for the temporary effacement of said memories);

5) An Ever-Tempting, Taunting, Beckoning Six-Foot Stretch of Rope;

6) Marshmallow Candy-Pops.

Now remember: you are holing up. So no cheating! You should only open the door for food delivery, prostitutes, or drug dealers. *Now let the languishing begin!*

●

By this point, you have no family, no job, no hope for the future, and even your most treasured childhood memories seem to wear on you like a Bjork record. More than likely, you are blacked-out drunk on a Tuesday afternoon, shirtless and wriggling in a pool of your own effluence. You may have shingles. You almost definitely have syphilis. And all you can wonder is why anyone would cancel *Becker*. Congratulations—you have successfully ruined your life. Now, if you can summon the will-power, try to right things and re-emerge into the society of others.

Or don't.

Honestly, we don't care either way.

SHORT ACCOUNTS OF TRAGIC OCCURRENCES (CONT.)

21

"Baby, I got to tell you: I never had leprosy. At the time it seemed like, to communicate to you what I thought needed communicating–well, it seemed like you could only understand it by believing I had leprosy; like the lie was actually truer than the truth was. But then our house was destroyed, and your brother fell in love with that goat, and it felt like everything but my torso was starting to fall apart. Baby, please don't stay angry at me. Not now, baby. Not when I'm dying of scurvy."

22

As a general rule, the mercenaries don't live. You can always expect this. If a mercenary lives, he is probably not a mercenary. He probably has some secret heart of gold that no one, least of all the other mercenaries, knows anything about. Chances are, the only reason he got wrapped up in such a half-baked scheme was to pay the debt on his grandfather's farm, pending a foreclosure that would have left him destitute. Probably, our man "the mercenary" knows nothing about guns, or interrogating the natives, or outflanking hostiles in the deepest bush. Probably, he does not lie awake at night, screaming the name "Fabrizio," and scratching at his eyes like they'd been bitten by sand fleas. Because, you see, he is not truly a mercenary, our man "the mercenary." That's just the part he plays, on television. Really, he's got that heart of gold. He's protected. He is one hundred percent protected right now.

THE OBITUARY WRITER'S STORY

I write five, ten obituaries a day, mostly for dead people.

In special circumstances, I'll do one pre-mortem. This will make things easier in the event of a plane-crash-or-mass-suicide-type rush. Only in very special circumstances will I do this, and only rarely. With your indulgence, I'd like to share one such "very special circumstance," by way of illustration. The account that follows happened a few years ago, in the Sayreville General Hospital. There was a woman there who–Aldrin? Allston? Alldred? I can't remember the woman's name. At any rate, she was very, very ill:

- So there's this old woman.
- She has this inoperably metastatic and mysterious tumor in her frontal lobe.
- It turns out this woman is a total quote/unquote fighter who just won't pack it in already. She lives and lives, this woman. Sort of selfishly, she lives.
- Eventually, this woman becomes so biblically old and thoroughly brain-ravaged she's essentially missing–like, mentally just gone ninety-three percent of the time.
- Soon enough this woman, for whatever reason, stops even evacuating her bowels. I mean, she absolutely will not defecate. Days go by. Weeks go by. Months go by while she's still being fed. Jealously, this woman holds her feces. She keeps it in and she keeps it in, and there's not even the slightest evidence of refuse. None of the woman's loved ones can coax her into going, and the whole thing becomes a kind of Christmas miracle. It's a sort of real-life display of conviction and will that a woman so weak and old and brain-damaged could abstain so long from shitting. Also, though, there is serious risk of abdominal trauma

because of all this. This risk concerns some people, but then they remember the brain tumor, and relax.

- Because of her age, the extensive brain damage, and the history of neurosurgery from increasingly frontal entry-points, this woman's got basically no face left. There's a sort of Picassoesque tableau of mounds and crevices where her face ought to be. It's textured by a lolling tongue, some mellowed sockets, asymmetrical, slit-like nostrils, visible stitching, scars, etc.

- It goes on like this. She gets to one year without moving her bowels, let alone having some kind of interpersonal exchange. She still makes these slight, aspirated puffs, though, whenever someone's around her.

- At some point in the third year of hospitalization, the alimentary/intestinal defenses just bust. Refuse of various shades and textures spills into the now-adjoining anatomical systems, causing all kinds of infection. Also, the tumor's as big as a second head, now, balanced on the first head.

- No one visits the old woman. She wouldn't care if they did. The end just seems impossibly nigh right now for the brain-damaged, deformed, malignant old woman. The doctors create some crude pool for betting, *viz* life expectancy. The daughters start discussing the woman in the distant past tense. De-odorizers are purchased in bulk.

- Eventually, the woman's family is prodded and pleaded into coming back to the hospital. The family resolves to "pull the plug," and are disappointed to learn that, because of the woman's miraculous autonomous breathing, there technically is no plug to pull. All of which is occurring some four and a half years after her initial admittance to the hospital, where she has racked up considerable expense for her children and well-wishers.

THE OBITUARY WRITER'S STORY

- Remember, now, that the woman is incredibly diseased all over. Her interiors (and increasingly, her exteriors) are an amorphous gel of tissue, infection, suppuration, and feces. She's got infections in her infections and tumors on her tumors. Somehow, the woman's organs dis- and re-entangle, making new and dynamic anatomies. There is no explanation for this. She's changing. Making herself new again.

- The woman is absolutely hideous through all of this. She becomes, now, an awful mass of tissue and muscle. Her non-face retreats below the tumor. Her arms become nubbins. She develops long phallic protuberances all along her spine. The woman recommences shitting from unexpected locales. She is shitting with comic frequency now. She lives.

- Euthanasia, though illegal, is seriously considered in a just-this-once-who-could-really-blame-us kind of way, both by family and doctors. No one dares, though, considering possible litigation.

- The woman—who is now more or less a tight, naked, sinewy ball; who is Caucasian-human-skin-colored, but otherwise bears no hallmarks of humanity—is removed from all IVs and monitors. With no nutrition, antibiotics, painkillers, or steroids, the woman continues to live.

- It is finally evident that she's eating herself from the inside out. She is losing mass and gaining refuse. Her domed new body (evidence suggests) is perfectly suited to auto-anthropophagi. Tissue's devoured; organs are eaten; bones are dissolved or excreted whole—all of this happens from the inside, invisibly. The woman begins to shrink. God, does she begin to shrink.

- After seven-odd years in hospital, and one year as a ball, the woman succeeds in eliminating her body. The husk of her form sort of recedes and vanishes, until all that's left of the biblically old woman are a bowel, a lung, and thirteen kilos of aromatic waste.

65

Albright! That was the woman's name. Vivian Albright, from Burlington, Maine. She used to raise terriers, I think.

SHORT ACCOUNTS OF TRAGIC OCCURRENCES (CONT.)

23

Abnormally large even from birth, Ludwig Wilhelm Bamberger stood six feet seven inches on the eve of his eighth birthday. He was scorned in the playground and hated at school. By the eve of his tenth birthday, Ludwig Bamberger stood four feet two inches, and is said to have claimed, "I hate nothing more than hunchbacks, now more than ever. They are ugly to behold, and dreadful to imagine. There is no meaner god than He Who Dreamt Up Hunchbacks, and I'm certain, Nana, there is only the one God."

"Yes," Nana said, "but why not blow out the candles, already?"

24

In his hospital cot, still trying to move his finger, Eddy wondered if it weren't, perhaps, a little too late for new beginnings. He had cheated on his girlfriend. He had shoplifted. He had sworn, fought, cheated, lied, insulted, scorned, degraded, abused, debased and double-parked more times than he could count. He had done all this without thinking. He had taken the Lord's name in vain, coveted his neighbor's wife, and had very probably, without ever realizing it, worshipped some kind of a graven image. On one particular occasion, Eddy had done most of these things at once, causing even the neighbor's wife to muddle up her rhythm and fall clamorously from bed, knocking Eddy square into his fatted, golden calf.

AFTER THE APOCALYPSE:
A SEQUEL, SORT OF

Αα ALPHA

After the fallout a lot of people die. The more infected eat the brains of the less infected, though their brains are eaten by zombie dogs. The dog brains are eaten by zombie cats, whose brains are eaten by zombie birds, whose brains are eaten by zombie worms, and so on. There's a new world order in place vis-à-vis brain-eating.

Ββ BETA

I wait it out in the shadow of an elm, near the summit of a mountain, to the west of a canyon. A long time passes before anything can happen. Then something happens.

Γγ GAMMA

About the thing that happens: without hopefully being glib, I will say that it is extremely bad. The kind of thing we would not believe could happen in a post-apocalyptic world where brains are getting eaten and dogs run off their leash. What happens is: out of nowhere there comes another apocalypse. That's two in a single calendar year. No one's too sure where it's coming from even, there being no infrastructure left. There are more toxins, more fallout. The zombies become zombie-mutants. The mutants become mutant-zombies. Skin colors turn a further shade of green.

Δδ DELTA

A lot of interspecies coupling–this is what happens in the wake of two apocalypses. First, the animals get smarter. Then the humans become stupider. Then the onset of radiation madness, in both humans and animals. Then the sexual congress part, both awkward and terrifying. Then a nice slow cigarette. Then a nap.

Εε EPSILON

Periods of gestation, unpredictable in length.

Ζζ ZETA

If there were still line charts, which there obviously are not, you might register a significant spike in births, all of them mixed-parentage. Apparently, fallout makes the sperm more adaptable. Apparently, also, it makes the ovum less selective. There's not much in the way of scientific precedent for this, but we all just try to "roll with it," seeing where things take us. There's a lot of what you might call "bold new challenges in the field of midwifery."

Ηη ETA

Animals of mixed parentage: you've got your centaurs, fauns, were-wolves, bear-wolves, minotaurs, beaver-men, satyrs. You've got your vertebrates bred with your invertebrates, your gastropods bred with your anthropods, your Caprinaes bred with your Leptocephales. None of the offspring are exactly gorgeous. Most appear to be glistening in slime. Few have the sort of purposive anatomy to keep them breathing a week. The ones that do live, breed.

Θθ THETA

I kill a baby dogmonster. It's dog and bird and I think a little Iowan potato farmer. It's spindly and stunted with thirteen legs and featherless wings. I kill it and bake it and season it with oregano, then I eat it for my own purposes—mostly out of hunger, but also out off love.

Iι IOTA

I wake one day and see a tiny grey rabbit rooting around my tree-house. It has the legs of a cow, and the eyes of something terrible hungering for blood. It is surprisingly adorable.

Κκ KAPPA

We enter a period I like to call "Interspecies Freak-Fest Number Two," wherein all the surviving offspring climb their way on top of one another. This brings more gestation, and further births, which ultimately leads us into "Interspecies Freak-Fest Number Three," and so on. There is a system at work, apparently.

Λλ LAMBDA

I am still alive somehow. I don't breed with anything and I don't interact, and I rarely bother to eat. I keep praying and praying and praying and praying, and one day a snake-thing falls out of the sky and crashes onto my hut. It has seven heads and three exposed hearts. "Is that you, God?" I ask it. "Have you come here to save us? Have you come here to show us the light? The lightning?"

Μμ MU

Interspecies Freak-Fest Number Four. In spite of much coaxing, I remain on the sidelines. Forever am I on the sidelines, watching.

Nν NU

I am the only human left, I think. I am the only human left in a violent sea of orgies. I fashion a hat, from tree bark.

Ξξ XI

There are apparently no species, now. Nothing alive bears a trace of its progenitors. There are no dogs or cats. There are no bats or badgers, owls or fish, monkeys or mice, snails or human beings. There is nothing even visibly descended from these things. What we have instead are variations on monstrosity. Creatures with a hundred filmy eyes. Creatures with rubbery toothless mandibles. Grey-green slabs of wriggling flesh. Some appear to have not much skin left. Some appear to be only skin. Some appear to be rendered inside out, their organs dangling like Christmas tree ornaments.

Oo OMICRON

There can be no more "Freak-Fests." There can be no more "Freak-Fests" because there is no more repose. What we have instead is a single ceaseless torrent of copulation. There are mountain-valleys filled with tireless humping. Open plains clogged with writhing shapes. Everywhere you look its superfluous limbs and gaping-wide orifices. Everywhere you look it's petting, stroking, pinching, sucking, grasping, thrusting, gnawing, licking, growling, moaning, or acts otherwise intended for the titillation of other monsters. I want so much to come down from my mountain—but can I? Can I really trust them? Can I really trust myself, down there, in the midst of all that flesh?

Ππ PI

These animals pause only to give birth. This could be fourteen minutes or forty five months. After partum, the mother resumes humping, while the infants stare on blinkingly. In any event, initiation will be swift. A child learns to copulate, or is trampled.

Ρρ RHO

Many, many years have passed. Twenty? Fifty? A hundred? More? My tree bark hat is disintegrating, even.

Σσς SIGMA

The animals retain their appetites. They eat, drink, defecate, bathe, nap, yawn, and scratch themselves, all without breaking their copulatory rhythms. They lead each other around like this–from shrub to tree to spring to bay, all the while still humping energetically. Nothing–and I mean nothing–will flag their frenzied baby-making.

Ττ TAU

I see a scaly grey whale-thing consuming its partner, mid-hump. I watch as this happens. It bucks and groans at the carcass, chewing between thrusts. Hours pass before it notices the limpness, and moves on.

Υυ UPSILON

I watch them: eat, fuck, sleep, fuck, birth, fuck, die. How long are their life spans now, these creatures–four years? One year? A single day? The Orgy Fields are littered with their corpses. Every generation, their lives become shorter.

Φφ PHI

I will come down from this mountain. I will come down from this mountain and bring order to the masses. How will I bring order? With the grace of our lord God. And how will God help me? Only he, in his wisdom, can be sure. But help, I am certain, is what he intends to do.

Χχ CHI

No. No, I will not come down from this mountain. I will not stick my neck out in that way. Not for these creatures, and not for any God. I will stay on my summit and make top hats and bowties. Always shall I be on this summit, making top hats and bowties.

Ψψ PSI

Time passes, and the things get lazier. With every generation, the flesh hangs looser, the eyes shift inwards, the skin looks more and more like pâté. On more than one occasion, a newborn arrives looking already decomposed. Like a tiny little lump of carrion. Like a tiny, horny, violent lump of carrion.

Ωω OMEGA

It finally happens. They hump and die, and die and hump until all that's left are the traces of bacteria. They simply de-evolve, the monsters. They strain and diminish and come apart–screwing themselves into boogery primordia. There is nothing now. There is literally just nothing.

   There is me myself. I myself.

   Whatever.

SHORT ACCOUNTS OF TRAGIC OCCURRENCES *(CONT.)*

25

(A)

His brain falls out and he scrambles to retrieve it. He's playing a game of poker, and trying to sort his cards, when his brain just plops out and he's forced to go all in.

(B)

A doctor arrives and heroically resuscitates him. Five years later, that handsome young doctor is none other than Jake Busey!

(C)

The man falls in love with a beauty queen who desperately wants to kill herself. Unfortunately, she has no limbs.

(D)

He mounts an expedition. But what kind of expedition? The Sherpas have enrolled in business college. The sailors are actually Chippendales. The camels are high-priced Venetian throw-rugs.

(E)

The man grows old and desperately wants to kill himself. He has the tools for it. He's still got all his limbs. He's able. He's willing. What is he, like, chicken or something?

(F)

Sometimes he feels like his brains are still moldering, somewhere below a poker table. What a terrible stain that brain must leave! Think about it! Think about people's shoes!

BACKWARD-PROJECTED COITUS PREVENTION

All we really knew was that we wanted him gone. Not dead or even kidnapped necessarily, but just–you know–cleanly absented from our day to day lives. And this is where it gets interesting.

You see, Lily and I began having these rousing hypothetical chats on whether the "unmaking of an individual through backward-projected coitus prevention"–through time travel–would in actuality be murder. We really had to ask ourselves: is contraception all that terrible? Or does it only become terrible when, with the benefit of time travel and twenty years foresight, you realize you don't especially like your own free-loading grown son?

Of course, answering this question started to seem all the more pointless after we'd answered the more glib and wistful questions of–namely–"has anyone around here got a time machine?" and "what are the going rates for rental of that time machine?" and "can I please, please book that time machine at its first availability?" As I said the whole thing started to seem pretty glib and pointless and pathetic, and Lil and I resolved to just stop with the science fiction, and to start patching things up with Jed, and to generally behave like tolerant and responsible parents. And this is where it gets interesting.

Because behaving like tolerant and responsible parents is exactly what we did not do. Because somehow every sputtered-off crack and morsel of backtalk made our fantasies more appealing; every little filial disappointment made our scenario seem more real. And the realer the scenario, the more pressing and confounding and ultimately compelling became the implications of that scenario. That we hated our son didn't seem so bad to us. That we felt poised to breech the fourth dimension, however; that we were prepared, as it were, to rip sperm from ovum at the very instant of conception–well, it raised a few unsettling questions: "What kind of parents would want this for their child?" etc. "Is he really so terrible?" etc. "Isn't this all, when you come to think of it, what with us having reared the little ungrateful so-and-so, really all our own faults anyway?"

Etc., etc., etc.

And it's when I recalled these kinds of dizzying complications that it seemed at once safer and easier and ethically more responsible, even, just to smother Jed in his sleep. And this is where it gets interesting.

Because, you see, shortly thereafter Jed died, mysteriously, in his sleep. We never asked him to leave the house for good or to please put on some underwear, because instead he suffered a fatal heart attack one week before his birthday–something which I don't mind telling you aroused a great deal of incredulity and suspicion and speculation on culpability, most of it directed toward Lily and I. Given all our chats regarding time-travel and individual-unmaking, we didn't even trust each other anymore, and there was generally a lot of guilt and shifting of blame and resentment flying around between us.

Until one afternoon several months later when I strolled into the homestead and came into our kitchen, and there on the floor sat my pink and naked wife. The sun was in her hair, and her hair was on her breasts, and her ankles were tucked in neatly below her thighs. All around her lay piles of scattered garbage: a cardboard box that used to contain doughnuts, a half a roll of silvery-grey duct tape, an unopened pair of rubber-grip wire cutters, a spool of copper wire, a stack of plastic cups, Styrofoam plates, a telephone cord, a hundred watt light bulb, an EZ Bake Oven, thread, twine, rocks, antennae, an analogue clock, a digital wrist watch, assorted shards of cheap plastic jewelry, paper clips, safety pins, scissors, glue, knives, forks, spoons, about half an eviscerated Commodore 64 (its plastic transistors strewn around everywhere), beer bottles, apple juice bottles, baby bottles, bourbon bottles, around ten nine-volt batteries, around twenty scattered thumbtacks, around five Tupperware brand sandwich containers, an apple, a pear, a banana, an uneaten bowl of high-fiber corn flakes (immediately to Lil's right), handcuffs, a flea collar, a no longer working Maytag mini fridge, quarter inch nails, half inch screws, and a creased, tan-yellow package of chewing gum.

I stood there looking on as she fit one piece of garbage into another piece of garbage with a kind of steely-eyed intensity. Her jaw went slack, and her pupils narrowed, and her head bent low to show her widening crown. The light bulb was fit into the plastic cup. The plastic cup was fit into the box. The cardboard box was fit into the computer, which was fit into the mini-fridge, which was covered in tape. She spread a wad of glue around the clock's back rim and pressed it to the fridge. She adjusted the time. She lifted the wristwatch. She picked up a fork.

And this is where it gets interesting.

ACKNOWLEDGEMENTS

Versions of "Short Accounts of Tragic Occurrences" numbers one, two, three, four and six appeared in *Matrix* magazine and *Pistol*. A version of "The Obituary Writer's Story" also appeared in *Pistol*. The story "Sayreville" was inspired by a comment made by Tony Hoagland in his *Best American Poetry 2003* interview. "Effective in Five Minutes" was inspired by a line in the George Saunders story "Ask the Optimist!" available in his collection *The Brain Dead Megaphone*.

Thanks to David McGimpsey for being an insightful editor and an illuminating teacher, and for having such faith in this book, even before it was written.

Thanks to Mike Spry for his brilliant feedback and tireless work, and for always being on hand with a beer and a kind word when I needed it.

Thanks to Mike Donovan, Brian Davis, Nathalie Edwards-Leroux, and Hillary Rexe for some invaluable feedback along the way.

Thanks to Steve Luxton and Philippe Barey for their hard work and interminable patience.

Thanks to Chelsey Ancliffe, Sarah Armstrong, Derek Evans, Jason Griffin, Rachel Levee, and Liz Tirovolas for their indulgence and overall awesomeness, and to Derek again for his ceaseless encouragement.

Thanks, with love, to Karen Dewart McEwen, for her incredible kindness and support, and for always managing to put up with me.

Thanks to my wonderful siblings and siblings in-law–Alison, Liam, Kit, Shannon, Fraser, and Meg–for all their friendship and enthusiasm, and to Kit again for proofing some of the science-related material in this book.

And finally, thank you to my loving and supportive parents, Mel and Rod McArthur, for more than I could possibly detail in this acknowledgements page. Your kindness has meant the world to me.

Oh, and my apologies to the real-life town of Sayreville, New Jersey. One day, I will actually visit you.

Nick McArthur grew up in Newcastle, Ontario, and currently makes his home in Montreal. His writing has appeared in *Matrix Magazine*, *Headlight*, and the *Pistol Anthology*, and he is a regular contributor to xtranormal.com.